WORLD AFTER SLEEP

AF516706

WORLD AFTER SLEEP

ANKIT HARSHBHAI MANIYAR

™

Bigfoot Publications
Because, there's a writer in everyone.

World After Sleep
Author : Ankit Maniyar

First Published by
Bigfoot06 Publications (OPC) Pvt. Ltd. B-10,12
Shree Shyam Palace,
Sector 4,5 Chowk, Old Railway Road,
Gurugram, Haryana (122001)
Website: www.bigfootpublications.in Email:
info@bigfootpublications.com

First Edition: November 2022
© Ankit Maniyar

ISBN Print Book - **978-93-90925-78-0**

All rights reserved. No part of this book may be reproduced or transmitted in any form or by any means, electronic or mechanical, including photocopying, recording, or by an information storage and retrieval system—except by a reviewer who may quote brief passages in a review to be printed in a magazine, newspaper, or on the Web—without permission in writing from the copyright owner.

Although the author and publisher have made every effort to ensure the accuracy and completeness of information contained in this book, we assume no responsibility for errors, inaccuracies, omissions, or any inconsistencies herein. Any slights on people, places, or organizations are unintentional.

Printed in India

INTRODUCTION

WORLD AFTER SLEEP, I have an observation. Every man is born in the world to do some work. Some natural events happen in the life of people, due to which some thought arise in their mind. And based on that idea, people have dreams about that since childhood. It is not necessary that every time those dreams will come true. But when we go to sleep, we create a world based on the thoughts running into our brain. In that world, the way we think and the feeling in that world is quite extraordinary and very pure. There is no trickery, fraud or any such thing in it. The life in that world is the true life according to one of the characters, while the life we are living now is fake.

This is a theory, which is not necessarily true. But at the same time, this book reveals one thing that it cannot be said that there is no word like 'feeling' in this world, but if you go very deep into it you can see it's necessitiy. May be I'm wrong in the concept of this world of sleep, but my observation, my imagination thinks something like this, which I put before you in the form of this book.

'Dad, why is there so much peace in this street? If same situation will be in our new home, I will be bored'. The little boy from the family of four, who was entering the new house with his belongings, sitting in the lorry, said looking out of the lorry.

'No, son, it's not like that. It's winter night, so everyone has gone to bed early, tomorrow morning you will make new friends in the neighborhood.'

'Yes Dad.' Excited, David slapped his sister Charlie on the head.

'Warner, you can explain to the children but every time you change houses just to solve a mystery. And again, this would mean that you have to spend for these processes.' Warner's wife Martina said .

Warner said. 'Marty, playing with these secrets is my passion. These secrets I have never read in a book. These secrets draw me to myself '. Warner replied quite instinctively.

'Warner, we have children. Who is responsible if anything happens to us?'

'Marty, trust my skills, my proficiency'. And there the lorry came and stood near the house. The roar of the lorry in the whole quiet area seemed to ruin the peace of whole area. In recent times, so much noise in the area has spread the feeling of fear in all the people around. Warner first got out of his lorry.

The mouth is long, the complexion is fairly white, the hair is neither long nor short, the nose is a little long in the symmetry of the mouth, the spectacles inthe eyes and the neatly maintained beard and mustache on the mouth were adding to the beauty. Warner's family was still inside. Warner was standing outside waiting for someone. This was the rule of all times.

'Hello, Mr. Warner I am Mr. Johnson. I just................................ '.

'Yes, you just called me and gave me information and asked for help.'

Warner said in the middle. 'Yes, Mr. Warner I will give you some information about me ....'.

Warner stabbed his cigarette and looked at Johnson, saying, 'Mr. Johnson, you have studied in Saint Mary from the first level to the fourth level, then your family changed the city so you have gone to another place. Rest of the school and college you did in the same city. You had a girl and a friend in college, and you had a relationship with her for six years. She left you as she fell in love with someone else. You put all your attention into work and today you own a very big company. Your family includes your wife and two children. Yes, why did you forget what your wife had to take today?

'What is the thing . Mr. Warner how do you know so much about me.'

'Mr. Johnson, there is reason behind everything. There is also a reason for this. We will talk about it later '.

Warner, there is a special reason for calling you here. The thing is ... '

'Mr. Johnson let us do that, you arrange for me to go inside my house'.

'Mr. Warner, I need to tell you about that home, that is why I have called you here. You have resolved so many secrets, and we hope that you can solve our problem too. This house is haunted . This house is the same when we all came to live, but from now on .... '

'Dad, how often I get a sleep.......... ' There was a sudden voice from inside.

'Yes son, let's go'. Warner replied to his son.

'Mr. Johnson, we can talk about that in the morning, and we are accustomed to live in such a house. You don't worry.'

'Okay as your wish Mr. Warner'.

'Well, Mr. Johnson, thank you'.

'Mr. Warner this is the key of your house.'

'Thank you Mr. Johnson'.

Warner took the vehicle inside the house. Got down from the vehicle and started watching the house from outside. The house was very large, there was a large garden around the house. Around the garden there was a boundry with white wall which was neither very high nor very low. Four rooms can be seen on the top of the house. Below was a hall, kitchen and a room.

'Dad has never seen such a big house.'

'Yes David, but you or Charlie is not going to be alone in this house, you have to stay with me or Marty.' Warner said while entering the house.

'Warner your these words scare me, this time you do not know where you risked our lives in search of mystery'. Marty said entering the house in the dark.

'What are you talking Marty, I can do anything for three of you. I will not let anything happen to you, and remember the time when you were not with me. This is the work in my life that I have supported. This is my earn for living Marty. Fear of death in people's mind is my earning. I have no fear of death or the situation, whtever that comes now is our income or a means of employment '.

The house was lighten up there 'Dad, this time I switched on the light a before you.'

'David, now the score of yours and dad to find switches in new houses are equal '. Charlie spoke in her small voice.

David was happy and started to tremble. 'No matter David I will win in the new home now.'

And everyone laughed and there was an atmosphere of happiness in the house.

'Marty, now keep these luggage in the room below. It is eleven o'clock in the night, so let's go to bed.' Warner said to Marty.

'Yes Warner, in this horrible house and in this horrible night, I feel the only way is to sleep'. Warner heard this and laughed.

"Dad let us all go to bed at the upper room today," David said and Charlie said yes to brother.

'Okay, son, one minute. Let me put this luggage inside and then we'll go to the room.'

'Warner, today we have to clean your bed in the same place, but tomorrow the whole housewill have to be cleaned. This house has been closed for a long time.'

'No Marty, this house was not closed for a long time'.

'How can you say'.

'From the cigarettes here. This cigarette has been just few days ago '. Warner saw the cigar lying in the room and said.

There was silence in the house and in the neighborhood. It may not be longbefore he falls asleep. There is a loud noise in the house.

'Marty, there's a lot of noise coming from the other room in the house, I don't have good feeling.'

Marty also sat up successfully, 'Warner I told you there must be something wrong in this house. Without that, you can't bring us people here. '

"Marty, this is not a topic for discussion right now. You guys stay here. I'll justgo outside and see."

'No warner, we should all gather outside in the garden and see.'

'I'll take Charlie, you take David.' All four come out in a hurry.

'Hey, the whole neighborhood has come out here, but everyone sees it from their homes. No one dares to come here."

'Not evryone are as crazy as we'.

"Now will you stop taunting me"

Warner gestures and calls everyone from the street. All are slowly coming to grips. There is a loud noise in the upstairs room. The lights of the room turn onand off, no shadow appears but there is a lot of noise. Marty and the two children cling to Warner. Neighbors are all standing in fear with their families. "Mr. Warner, this is the thing for which I have called you here. For two hours every night, this scene is very

common for the people here."

'How long has this been happening?'

'We've been experiencing this for almost last one month'. "It happens only for two hours during night?"

'Yes, this sound is only for two hours at night.'

An object came straight down from above and a scream was heard from upstairs. Immediately hearing that people left the house.

'Mr. Warner, it's not right for you to be in that house right now. You can go to my house tonight and start your work tomorrow.'

'Mr Johnson, thank you, you take Marty and the two children to your house, I really need to stay in that house today'.

'Warner this is what happes always, you fight with death there and I can never sleep comfortably.'

'Marty, don't worry, you know my job.'

'Yes Warner it is fine but I'll come with you, let's leave the kids at Mr. Johnson's house'.

'Yes, let's go ...'

'Johnson, please take care of both my children tonight.'

'Mrs. Marty, don't worry. If you people go to this building for us at the risk ofyour life, I can take care of your children.

'Thank you, Mr. Johnson.'

'David - Charlie go with Uncle to his house and don't bother him too much'. Both David and Charlie left with Mr. Johnson. And all the neighbours also slowly went to their homes. Marty and Warner were the only remaining in the area. The empty road was like talking cold-cold wires in the winter. Cool breeze and empty street and a haunted house in front.

'Marty, what do you think of sitting in the garden and drinking hot coffee when we are alone in such a cool weather?'

'We are not the only two here, we are three.'

Warner looked around and said, 'Who is the third?'

'Your ghost against this.'

'Hey, the ghost only come for two hours, let him do his job, let's have a coffee.'

Marty stood outside in the garden for two minutes. And Warner went inside to get coffee. Marty was looking at the house with a scary look from outside. Warner came out with a thermos of coffee and two cups. In the garden, both of them came and sat in aplace that was small and comfortable. The coffee smoke in the cup was soothing, the cool breeze and this soothing road gave a pleasant experience.

"What more could you want than such a nice coffee, with you, and such

a nice atmosphere," said Warner, taking coffee in one hand and Marty in the other. "Warner, I know your way of working. I know you already know all about thiscase." Marty said with a look of concern on his face.
"Marty, I'm talking to you here with love and you're talking about work, then don't tell your friends I'm not romantic." Warner said kissing Marty's hand.
'No Warner, it's not like that, I worry about you, you save us and other people in all thesedangers but your life is always in danger. And you also know, I have no one in this world except you.'Marty said placing her head on Warner's shoulder.
Marty's head was on Warner's shoulder, the two of them holding each other's hand, as if they are a new couple. A hot sip of coffee was more auspicious in such a cold environment. Warner's flying hair, long nose. The curiosity in his eyes, the love for his family was something special on his face today. They were both sitting and Marty kissing him and rubbing one of his shoulders. They both fell asleep in each other's arms. In the morning, when the rays of the rising sun fell on both of their faces,they lost their sleep.
'Marty, let's go inside and put the things in order first and do some cleaning and make the house livable.'
'Yes Warner, the same thing has to be done first'. Marty said as he straightened his clothes.
'Yes Marty today is Sunday also and all the people of this area will be at home today, so we have to do something to meet everyone'.
"Then let's do this, let's clean up here and then call all the people in our areaand discuss with tea and snacks."
'The idea is very good, such a good idea can only come to my wife'. Warnerkissed him on the head with love.
'Just don't add too much butter'. And with love on his head, Marty stood up. 'Let the people of the area get up, the house has to be cleaned first'. And they both got up and went inside.
'First let's see all your stuff, arrange it properly.' Marty said as he quickly entered the house.
'Yes, first we will arrange your belongings and then start cleaning the place".
Warner turned on the light as soon as he entered.

To the surprise of both, the whole house was clean. Not a single particle of dust is visible inside the house.
'Warner, I don't feel like living in this house anymore. Who cleaned this house when you and I were out there', Marty screamed and hugged Warner passionately.

'No Marty, there is no need to be afraid, this ghost has made our job very easy.'Warner said, patting Marty's head.
'Warner what are you talking about, this is a ghost why don't you understand.'Marty looked at Warner angrily and shouted.
'Marty you understand, this ghost has cleared the house for us and signaled us to stay here. Not all ghosts are bad, what is the reason to be afraid of ghosts. A ghost is none other than a dead human being. I see no reason to be so afraid of ghosts.' Warner said with great ease, smoothing his hair with ease. A hope was visible in that eye that maybe Marty would believe by saying so much in one breath. putting a cigarette in his mouth with a twinkle in his eye.
'Warner, how can you say this so easily?' Marty said with wide eyes and a strange glow.
'Marty before I let any fear enter me, I ask myself many questions. Before any fear weakens me, I weaken it by my logic. Think about why you people are afraid of ghosts, because ghosts are invisible, your people's idea of ghosts is very strange. Scary face, upside down legs and don't know what. A ghost to me is a restless soul. Who has only one desire, that is to live that desire, to live that dream.' Warner said leisurely puffing on his cigarette.
Marty calmed down a bit. 'So now what is the next thought in this matter.' Marty said calming down a bit.
'Marty I don't know, I can say one thing for sure, after this case I will prove a truth to the world that will shock the world.' Warner muttered something down below.
'Marty in the world it is not always what we think, the desires in the mind is never going to be fulfilled, life is always going to end with some unfinished story. No one's story will ever be finished. And that unfulfilled desire is the birth of a new beginning. And in the second birth that story continues. But often the desire is so strong that it is difficult to control it. Andthe time between the old birth and the new birth which cannot be lived it comes to fulfill that desire with an empty soul without a body. It is not a religion to be afraid of a hungry soul.' Warner very calmly explained to Marty.
'Warner, how can you take this matter so comfortably. I have read in that bookabout souls that how once the soul leaves the body, it forget all the relationship here and is working for the ghost demon and it's

only aim is to gather more and more souls.'
Warner is looking at souls from human feeling, human spirit, human intelligence which is not possible. As soon as the body is placed, the person leaves everything here. Marty gasped with a breath, his silver mouth a glimpse of question marks from fear. The sweat on the face was coming downon the body, it was clearly visible in the eyes.
Warner calmly took his cigarette in his hand and said, 'Marty, for me, satisfying souls is the greatest virtue, but here we do not think so. This is the case outside of souls.'
Marty gets upset and says what Warner is trying to say, this is not a soul upthere.
Warner said with a little smile, 'I will tell you in time. Now let's arrange thegoods.'
Marty began to arrange the same with an odd price. Warner opened his bag and started taking out his old belongings one by one. Marty comes there in that room and looks at Warner and says, 'HeyWarner, why are your eyes down.'
'Marty time flows like water and people change with time', says Warner. 'But that time leaves some memories in our life. Even today I remember those days when my parents were alive. Even today I feel their lack somewhere.' Without saying a word, Marty gives Warner a much needed hug. Warner recovers after a while.
Seeing Marty lost in some thought, Warner asks, 'What happened, why is Marty in such a thought.'
Marty looks at Warner with somewhat questionable expression. Marty's piercing eyes, perfectly arranged eyelashes, eyes widened with questioning expression, well-arranged hair were asking many questions to Warner.
'Marty you can ask, anything you want.'
Marty asks him, 'Warner, why did you cry so much remembering your parents even though you know so much about the afterlife. Why did I remember it so much today instead of any other day? I am surprised by this. Why did you suddenly started crying today remembering your parents who never used to cry.'
Warner looks down for a moment and then starts speaking in his own voice, 'Marty, the real owner of the place we're standing across from can tell you that.Get ready soon, we have to go to meet him now.'
'Warner, I'm too scared to get ready without you being in this room.'

'Marty, don't be afraid, this house is very holy, I'm sitting right here.'
'Warner what shall I wear today, if you say, how about this pink dress.'
'Oh God, I was afraid to go to bath now. But the dress has to be selected and worn only. Marty remember after your marriage when you were standing in front of the mirror for the first time and asking me about the dress like this.'
'Yes, Warner, I don't know how time is passing, it still seems like yesterday.' Grasping Marty's shoulder lovingly, Warner grabs Marty from behind. Warner we will always be together.
'Yes, why does Marty say that?'
'Warner, I am very afraid of the way you are working on this case.'
'No Marty, trust me my dear.'
'I have full confidence in you Warner, but not in this situation.Circumstances always separates a person from someone whom they love.'
'No Marty, man always takes other people's things as his own, and then he is afraid of losing because he knows that this thing or person is not mine and because of that he is more afraid.'

'Warner you know you are a very smart man you know everything.' As soon as she said this, Marty patted him gently and hugged Warner dearly. As if two lovebirds met each other today and forgot about the whole world. The sun seems to be meeting the ground on the horizon. The water in the ocean seems to be reaching the shore today. It is as if two hearts are meeting with a completely pure mind without any lust.

And just then, there was a knocking sound from the opposite room again. Marty was separated from Warner with a jerk.

'Warner. What's that sound?, Warner this horrible sound is tearing my ears part. I have crushes in my mind. As if an arrow is coming out of the heart.'

Warner came out of the bedroom door with Marty in his arms when there was a loudknock on the door in the opposite room, and both men startled back again.

Looking at the clock, it was exactly seven o'clock in the evening and both of them came back down outside the house. Looking them, everyone came out on the street and stood. But Warner raised his hand and signaled that we were both safe. Everyone was standing in the distance watching, Warner and Marty were standing down. It was a very scary atmosphere, the whole neighborhood was quiet again. The sound of birds at night was making the atmosphere more terrifying. Warner signaled all the people of the neighborhood to go inside, and told his two boys not to worry from a distance, both brothers and sisters, mom and dad, were coming running but Warner stopped them there, with signal. And both people understood and went back.

Warner came out and loudly announced that we are having a meeting at the Moholla Secretary's house within an hour.

After saying this,Warner went to Marty. Marty was looking at Warner with a very serious face. She was trying to find something in Warner's eyes. Marty was trying to get answers to her many questions, but she was not getting any answers from Warner.

'Warner I think you are not sure about this case, I always see you in all cases and I get the answer that you have the way in that case but I don't think so in this case.'

'You are right Marty, I tried to make many connections of this soul while we were in this case but no, I have not been able to find a single connection yet.'

Hearing this, Marty's white face and the light point slipped on the braid hanging in it and landed on his face. And the mouth opened in surprise, and in a little loud voice said, 'Warner, what are you talking about? Are you telling me that you haven't got anything yet? We were sitting inside without having any hint of dangers that can come anytime, what is going on.'

Warner grabs Marty's shoulder and calms her down,'Marty, calm down, we arehaving a meeting to resolve this. Everyone will be waiting for us, let's go.'

'Warner for me this matter is more serious than any of past cases.'

'Marty it's really serious, based on my experience when we people were inside I tried to get many clues but I couldn't succeed. So I can say that this case is different from all my previous cases.'

'Warner there would be a link from which we could reach to some conclusion.'

'Yes Marty, it is not one thing but two things and I am calling this meeting to discuss that. We will all be waiting in the meeting', as Warner goes, and both walk out.

'Warner I can't close the door of the house, can you just come.'

'Marty don't worry I'm coming.' Warner goes to close the door, Marty watching him from behind.

In the dark of night, Warner walks slowly home, away from Marty. Marty was looking around with a frightened face, the whole neighborhood was under a scary atmosphere, this silent house on one side, the loud creaking sound in this silent street was making the atmosphere even more terrifying.

Warner suddenly reached the door and went inside without closing it. And Marty screamed loudly. At the same time, all the people gathered at the house of Mohalla, secretary came out, and Warner comes out of the house just as he runs towards Marty.

And the whole neighborhood is standing outside his house.

Warner had a cigarette in his mouth, his mouth expression was that nothing had happened. There was a sense of pride on his white face, the pride of having mastered what the world fears. Lightly flowing hair, very thin mustache on the face, slowly growing beard were making his attitude more dense.

Everyone's eye were on Warner, the darkness was very quiet in the neighborhood. The chirping sound of birds was echoing in the atmosphere. A strange fear was visible on everyone's face.

'Warner, what happened, why did you walk in suddenly?'

'Marty I'm fine as I went to close the door and saw an earring lying by the stairs. And this Kundal, Marty is not yours and I think it is from a long time ago. I see this as some evidence for the case.' Warner was slowly going to put it in his pocket. There, aloud sound echoed in the atmosphere, as if there was a breach in the calm atmosphere.

There was a loud noise in the quiet house and it was coming from the window in the upper room, and everyone was startled. A very unfamiliar voice came out, 'Alvin give me back my coil, Alvin you left me but this is the last sign of Vegas you can't take it away.'

Alvin, hearing this screams in the air, everyone ran out of the house.

Warner, Marty and all the people of the neighborhood ran and reached the house of the secretary of the society. Someone was sitting on the sofa, half of the people were sitting on the table.

The whole house was buzzing with noise, people were talking to each other in fear. Warner andMarty finally enter the house and the

atmosphere is completely calm.
Warner calmly took the glass of water in his hand and slowly started drinking it one sip at a time.
All eyes were on Warner. In a very quiet environment, Warner was sitting on a sofa and Marti was standing calmly supporting him on his shoulder.
'Warner sir, what is going on, how will you solve this.'
'See I find this case a bit different, initially I didn't had any evidence in this case, but now I have a lot of evidence that can be said in this case, like the voice only comes between seven and nine, second is Kundal, third is Alvin and The fourth proof is Vegas. I can connect these four links with each other and reach the result. Secretary sir, who lived in this house before, if I want to see the details of this house.'
'Warner sir, this building is empty since this neighborhood was built, but if you want to see the details, I will go to the government office tomorrow morning and get it. And you and Marty sleep here today, no need to go to that house.'
And rest of the people slowly went to their homes in fear.
In the house now were Secretary M's wife, Warner Marty and his two boys. Both boys hugged Warner and Marty together. Warner and Marty were loving their children. The secretary and his wife politely showed Warner and Marty their room.
After playing with the children for a while, Warner and Marty went to sleep in the room. Marty was very tired and fell asleep as soon as she went to bed, Warner was in a deep thought standing by the window in the room still looking at the building opposite.
More than an hour passed, and Warner heard something muttering. He suddenly turned back and looked, but Marty was fast asleep and babbling inher sleep.
'Today is my first flight after becoming a pilot.' Warner heard this and remembered the conversation between himself and Marty. Marty's early dream was to become a pilot, but for some reason it could not be fulfilled and today she was living the same thing in her dreams. Warner slowly walked over to the window and sat next to Marty. He was looking straight at Marty. Marty was flying as a pilot in sleep. A strange happiness was visible on her face, a unique smile that Warner always wanted to see . But he never got to see that happiness. Which was now

could be seen on her face.

Warner thinks for two minutes.

Slowly caressing Marty's cheek. Warner was lost in thought, as per his nature he began to think a little more deeply on this matter. He started searching something in his mobile and his facial expression changed. And Warner stood up straight and started walking towards the house.

It is a dark black night, the nightis very quiet, the peace in the night is such that it makes anyone's heart tremble. The sound of night birds, the barking of dogs, was making the atmosphere more serious. Warner was going home with a firm footing. Once inside the main door of the house, Warner resumed his inspection.

He is sitting down in the grassy area looking for something. Slowly he goes inside. And the night passes like that.

Rising and falling is a natural sequence of events. When the first ray of the sun falls on this stream. A new day always brings something new in a person's life. Someone celebrates their success, someone sees their failure on the same day, someone moves ahead with their dreams of a new beginning in the same light. One loses one's logo in the same ray. One welcomes many new people into the same ray. Today's morning was a shock for Marty.

When the first rays of the morning fell on her face, she suddenly got up and saw that Warner was not in the room.

And all of a sudden she started looking for Warner from side to side. But Warner was nowhere to be seen, and Marty's anxiety began to grow, and she began to worry about Warner.

She wasn't able to find him anywhere. Marty comes out of the room and started looking for Warner all over the house but there was no sign of him anywhere. Marty comes out in the hall, but still wasn't able to find him. The secretary's wife comes out.

And asks Marty what happened. Marty says Warner is nowhere to be seen. The secretary, his wife and Marty all three come out of the house. Normal life was going on outside. Sun was showing his strength. The three people left the house and went to the side of the house to find Warner.

Standing outsidethe house, Marty screamed worriedly,'Warner, Warner, where are you? What does he do inside the house? Come out soon are you fine? I told you to return Kundal yesterday, but you refused. Warner answer me. Where are you? . The quiet atmosphere was resounding with excitement.

Warner came out of the house and gestured to Marty to be quiet. A strange smile was visible on his face, as if he had overcome some kingdom, as if some victory had been done. The tiredness of the whole night was not visible on his face, he had the same cigarette on his face, as if nothing had happened. The hair was blowing in the air by itself. There was a different kind of brightness on the face.

Marty came forward and gave a vigorous slap and said to Warner, 'Warner, what do you think of yourself, you are God? What do you think of you are? You can solve everything. What do you know, how many people are responsible for you. Both of my children. You understand, what do you understand? We know that you are not afraid of death, we know that you are above all this. But we people care about you, it will make a lot of difference if you die , you are more important for us, you understand?'

Warner hugged Marty without giving any reaction. After a while Marty calmed down,the secretary asks Warner,

'Warner sir are you fine, you should not go alone inside that house.'

'No, secretary sir, I am fine and the case has also been solved. There is no ghost inside, we people have to handle this thing very comfortably.'

'It doesn't seem understandable, what do you want to say?'

'It means that this is not a ghost or its dizziness, this is the dizziness of the relationship within. A person living here, Alvin, left his mother here after the death of his father. And for so many years, he was making the same noise here, and you people thought he was a ghost. Last night I did all these penances and called Alvin here and sent him to the hospital with his mother and they are both safe and now not even a single sound will come from your house. And we people can also live here now.'

AFTER FEW MONTHS

Few months have been passed. It's Sunday, hot tea is on the table, Warner and Marty are at home today. Warner is working onsomething on the laptop. Marty is sitting in front of Warner.

'Warner I don't understand why we are not going to any case right now. After the last case, we are here and have not gone anywhere for any case and you are working on laptop only. I don't understand anything.'

'Marty you remember the last case, that case is over there but that case is not over yet I am going to prove a very big theory on this case.'

'Theory, what theory.'

'This theory is from a different world. And the idea of this theory and the case that I have solved is because of you.'

'Me,I don't understand. What did I do?'

It is about the time when we people used to sleep in the secretary's house. You were also sleeping then, and you were muttering something in your dreams. I heard that you were flying a plane as a pilot in your dreams.

'What is Warner talking about? I was flying as a pilot?'

'Yes, and I have never seen the happiness on your face during the whole life' 'Yes, but how is it related to anything with this?'

'Let me explain, how many people live in this world, and all the people have some desire which we cannot fulfill for some reason or the other. And that desire remains unfulfilled.'

'That's right too.'

'Yes, taking it a little further, at night when we sleep we go to a different world, what we call dreams are not dreams in my opinion but a different world. In which all your thoughts, all your dreams are fulfilled. The world is yours and you have gained everything you wanted. And there we are quite happy or sad, but whatever feeling we have is complete in that world and always in extreme level . Whatever of sadness, happiness, love, fear, it means the world of imagination. This is the real world, not the world of imagination. The world we are living in now is wrong.

'What are you talking about, you mean we are alive when we sleep.'

'Yes, that world is not real when we are awake. And when you sleep, the real world starts.'

'But because of that, how was that case solved?'

Warner explained his point that Alvin spent his childhood in a very good home. Big house, dad's big business, mom's love at home, good school. A child raised in a rich family with a golden-spoon. Husband and boy became the world for mother, for them she left her work. And devoted her whole life in the name of family. Thinker Marty How difficult it is to dedicate your career to someone else. She put all her dreams and life behind Alvin. Then her husband left this world after some time. And Alvin's mom was deprived of a support or you can say the basis of living. Now Alvin was the only basis of living for her. Alvin is slowly growing up until his mother took over the entire business. Paying full attention to Alvin, studying him and listening to everything. Her life was limited till Alvin now. Alvin was growing up slowly, after finishing school he was now slowly reaching college and was also helping in the business, then like everyone's life found a girl, got married and settled down. But the quarrels were gradually increasing in the house.

And Alvin went to live elsewhere with his wife. It was unbearable for his mother to bear this shock and slowly the loneliness of the house was eating her away. Once she was asleep, and after going into a slumber, she went into his own real world, just like you, where Alvin was with him, and that world she found most loving. But when morning came, they come out of that world. And again the lack of Alvin was eating her away. The same thing happen repeatedly when the night falls, now she started to like the world of sleep more than this world in which where Alvin was near him.

But in this world you cannot nourish the body . It is very necessary to come out of that world into this world. The power that was lost. And even after coming to this world, they were living in the same world due to which all theseproblems were happening.

'Oh that's interesting Warner, I mean the whole world is crazy according to you.' 'Yes, it is crazy because everyone has some desire in their mind which cannot be fulfilled in this world, that's why the whole world is living in another world within itself which is called the **WORLD AFTER SLEEP**.'